Little Tigers

Jo Weaver

Hodder
Children's
Books

Dawn was breaking in the jungle.

Two little tigers, Puli and Sera, were excited to
start their day. But Mother Tiger was worried.
Last night she had heard men and dogs on the
jungle paths near their home. It wasn't safe any more.

"My little ones," she said,
"we need to find a new home."

"I know somewhere safe," said Sera.
"The frogs told me about it."

"Then you show us the way," said her mother,
and the tigers left their den for the last time.

Sera led them away from the danger, through the chattering jungle to where the river plunged over a cliff.

"Over here!" she said and they leapt
behind the rushing water.

On the other side of the waterfall was a cool, damp cave. Little beads of water glistened on their fur.

"Isn't it lovely!" said Sera.

"Lovely for a frog, maybe," said her mother kindly. "But too wet for us tigers. We need somewhere warm and dry."

"Then I know just the place!" said Puli. "The monkeys are always talking about it."

"Follow me!" he called, leaping into a tree and scrambling up the branches.

Up and up the three tigers climbed,
high into the safety of the jungle canopy.

"Look how warm and dry it is!" said Puli.

"Yes," agreed his mother, "and it's great
for monkeys. But it's a very long way to fall.
Tigers need to sleep on the ground. Let's keep looking."

Together they roamed the deepest parts
of the jungle, exploring its secret places.

Mother Tiger was growing more anxious.
The day was passing and they still hadn't
found a new home.

Puli spotted a cave in the rocks.
"What about here?" he said.
"This looks perfect."

But inside it was full of stinging, biting creepy crawlies.

"It's perfect for insects, but not for us," sighed their mother.

The little family moved off again, still searching for somewhere safe.

"It's lovely and sheltered in here," said Sera, looking under the roots of an old tree.

But a big python slithered from the branches.
The tigers slunk away.

The night was drawing in and they still had
nowhere safe to sleep. Mother Tiger was very worried.

Then she remembered. There was one place where
no one would find them . . .

It was somewhere close by, but could she find it in time?

"Wait here, little ones," said Mother Tiger.
She gave them a loving nuzzle and disappeared
into the shadows.

"Will she come back soon?"
whispered Puli.

"I hope so," said Sera, huddling
close to her brother.

At last they heard their mother's voice.

"I'm up here," she called. "Don't be scared."

The cubs followed her up a crumbling
staircase into an old stone temple
overgrown with creepers.

Inside, it was warm and dry and safe.
"Our own secret den!" said Sera.

"And we can see the stars!" said Puli, curling up next to his sister.

Mother Tiger watched over them, listening to the familiar sounds of the jungle at night.

"Goodnight, my little ones," she whispered.
"Welcome to your new home."

But Sera and Puli were already fast asleep.

For Rowan and Felix,
with all my love x

First published in 2019 by Hodder Children's Books
© Jo Weaver 2019

Hodder Children's Books
An imprint of Hachette Children's Group
Part of Hodder & Stoughton
Carmelite House
50 Victoria Embankment
London, EC4Y 0DZ

1 3 5 7 9 10 8 6 4 2

HB ISBN: 978 1 444 93752 7
PB ISBN: 978 1 444 93753 4

An Hachette UK Company
www.hachette.co.uk

www.hachettechildrens.co.uk

FSC
www.fsc.org

MIX
Paper from
responsible sources
FSC® C104740